MIKE PAYNE

Charlie's Ark ®

Illustrated by Adam Pescott and Mike Payne

AUSTIN MACAULEY PUBLISHERS™

LONDON • CAMBRIDGE • NEW YORK • SHARJAH

A CIP catalogue record for this title is available from the British Library.

ISBN 9781035846290 (Paperback)
ISBN 9781035846306 (Hardback)
ISBN 9781035846313 (ePub e-book)

www.austinmacauley.com

First Published 2023
Austin Macauley Publishers Ltd®
1 Canada Square
Canary Wharf
London
E14 5AA

This book is dedicated to my dear and valued friend
Arthur Maxfield

Foreword

Charlie's Ark is about a five-year-old boy and his magical toy box. The toy box is in the shape of an ark and contains many animals which are magically brought to life by a secret 'Wordspell'.

The stories are in rhyme and have a moral message. They are a throwback to traditional values and there is a warmth and truth in all the stories which will resonate with everyone. They remind adults of a time when they themselves were children.

Whether young or young at heart, you will not fail to be utterly enthralled by Charlie and the adventures he has with his magical animals in *Charlie's Ark*.

Contents

Prologue

Sixty or so years ago there lived a little girl who had a passion for her toy animals. She kept them in a cardboard box, which wasn't ideal, but then she had an idea. She asked her father, who was a carpenter by trade, to make her a magical toy box in the shape of an ark for them all to live in. Her father loved his daughter dearly, and decided he would make the finest, most beautiful toy box ark there had ever been.

Early one morning, as he entered his workshop and saw the ark that he was working on there on his bench, he gave a sharp intake of breath. The sunlight was streaming through the little window and was dancing and playing on the blade of one of his chisels. The light shone directly onto the ark with wondrous colours of the rainbow. He looked at the ark and said to himself, "This ark is not an ordinary toy box…no, I do believe it is magical." He finished it that very day. He worked and worked, sanding and polishing the walls, but the last thing he did was to put a little scrap of paper into the roof. It wasn't just any old scrap of paper though, for on it he had written a few simple words…

The next morning, he presented it to his precious daughter. The little girl was thrilled with it and jumped up and down with delight. It was everything she could have imagined it to be. She hugged her father really tightly, and both had tears of happiness in their eyes.

Now an old lady, she remembers that moment as if it was yesterday and, one afternoon, she made a decision. She would give the ark to her only grandson Charlie as a gift. She knew he loved animals, and that he would treasure it as much as she had. She would also pass on that little scrap of paper to him…and the magical secret.

Later that day she presented it to him, and he was thrilled, just as she had been. Whilst Charlie was hugging her, her mind went back to when she had hugged her father in exactly the same way and, smiling, she pressed the little folded scrap of paper into Charlie's hand.

There was a question in his eyes, but she put her finger to her lips and said, "Ssshhh." Then, speaking really quietly, she said, "Only read this out loud when you are with your ark and you are on your own. It's a 'Wordspell'." She leaned in even closer and whispered, "After saying these words, magical things happen."

Charlie nodded, his eyes wide with excitement, and put the little piece of paper into his trouser pocket.

After his grandmother had gone home, Charlie asked his mum to take the ark up to his playroom in the loft so he could play with it. He knelt in front of it and was so excited he started to shiver a little. What did his grandmother mean about magical things happening? And what was a 'Wordspell?' He reached into his pocket for the scrap of paper and carefully unfolded it. It was a patchy brown colour and looked very, very old. He stared at the words, glad that he was good at reading and, taking a deep breath and trembling, he said the words out loud: "In this ark, right here, right now, animals awake, come alive somehow…"

The ark began to tremble and shake and lots of coloured lights came on inside and started shining out of the windows! There was a murmuring and, all of a sudden, the roof of the ark started to raise itself into the air, lifted by a wonderful rainbow! Before Charlie realised what was happening, all the animals started clambering out! There must have been about 30 of them, and they stood right in front of Charlie on the playroom floor. They all had rainbow-coloured manes and tails and top-knots on their heads, and Charlie gulped. He took another deep breath.

"Hello…" he said. "I'm Charlie! Pleased to meet you!"

The animals all smiled, and some of them giggled, and they said in a variety of voices, "Yes, we know who you are! We'd better introduce ourselves!"

The names came thick and fast. Spud was the hippo, Buss was the lion, Putty was the monkey… Charlie was having trouble trying to remember all the names, as there were so many!

When all the animals had introduced themselves, they got down to the serious business of playing some games. Charlie wondered just what his grandmother had given him. The ark was magic! The animals were magic! This was the best thing that had ever, ever happened to him, ever.

Charlie's Ark

Charlie is five and a great little boy
Who loves to play with his favourite toy.
It's not a car, and it's not a plane,
It's not toy soldiers, and it's not a train.

It's a sort of boat where inside is kept
The very biggest and best secret.
It's just you and me, so I'll tell you now;
I'll tell you why, and where and how.

But don't tell anyone, or make a fuss.
This secret is between the two of us.
It's nothing horrid and it's nothing bad,
But the best thing Charlie has ever, ever had.

Now Charlie's parents know about this toy,
For they've seen his face lit up with joy.
I shall say it quietly, so no one hears:
The boat's full of animals...they've been there for years.

There's a horse and a lion, a hen and a cat,
A zebra, a pig, and a duck that's fat.
There's quite a few so don't be upset,
For if I list them now you'll forget.

All have names like Tumble, you see.
There's Fizzy and Spud, Buss and Pee.
So pretty soon I think you'll know
Charlie's Ark and who told you so.

The Rainbow

There's a magical rainbow in the sky
The colours are special, I'll tell you why.
Pink is for sharing,
Yellow is for giving,
Blue is for caring,
Green is for living,
Lilac is for loving,
and so it must be true.
This rainbow is alive
in both me and you!

Hide

It was a day like any other day,
And after breakfast Charlie decided to play .
He went to his playroom and opened the door.
There, in the corner, was the ark on the floor.

He smiled when he saw it, delight in his eyes.
He closed the door softly and went to his prize.
I'll tell you now what Charlie said there,
But don't tell a soul! Promise and swear!

Charlie spoke carefully, slowly and soft,
Kneeling before his ark in the loft.
"In this ark, right here, right now,
Animals awake, come alive somehow!"
There was a soft glow and a rush of warm air,
From within the ark a stirring somewhere.

Slowly but surely Charlie could see
The lid of the ark raise magically.
Charlie held his breath, for the animals stood in line
There in front of him for the second time!

Charlie then said, "Let's play a game.
What would you like? Give me a name!"
"Hide and seek!" they shouted as if they were one.
Hide and seek it was, and in a blink it had begun.
So who would hide and who would seek?
Charlie had puzzled over this for nearly a week.
Spud the hippo would be the one,
The other animals seeking could have the fun.

Charlie closed his eyes and counted to twenty.
It should be enough time. It should be plenty.
Spud raced away just as fast as he could,
Across the floor, but he slipped on the wood.
Falling and tumbling at a remarkable pace,
He came to rest by an old bookcase.

This gave him an idea and with a quick look
He squeezed himself behind a big book.
It took a while, for he is quite fat,
But he finally did it and breathless just sat.
Now all this excitement was too much to bear,
And within seconds he fell fast asleep right there.

"Twenty!" Charlie shouted, "Coming, ready or not!"
The animals rushed around, only Ben had lost the plot.
He couldn't remember the game or even the day
Until reminded by his good parrot friend Jay.
The animals searched and searched and still
They couldn't find Spud. Their result was nil.

Charlie grew tired and the animals too.
And eventually the game proved too much to do.
They returned to the Ark and Charlie replaced the lid.
Never knowing where Spud was or where he hid.
"So what happened next?" I hear you all say.
Well, I'll tell you my friends, but another day!

Seek

Spud the hippo awoke from his sleep,
Opened his eyes and risked a quick peep.
He was wedged behind a very large book
And by a bookcase, he saw from this first look.
But why was he there? Why not in the Ark?
Was Charlie having a joke? Was he there for a lark?

Oh yes, he remembered, they were having a game.
He remembered hiding, but oh what a shame!
Must have fallen asleep in this very spot.
Everyone had gone – they must've forgot!
There was no Charlie to say the magic 'Wordspell',
So he could fully move and use his voice as well.

What was he to do? He could but wait
And hope they found him before too late.
Back in the Ark the animals were aware
That one of their number just wasn't there.
It was unlike Spud to go missing, he was always around,
But they searched high and low – he couldn't be found!

Normally they fell asleep and rested in peace,
Until Charlie would come and provide their release.
But, tonight was different and although lying still,
Thoughts turned to Spud – could he be ill?
The minutes pass slowly at times such as these;
The hours ticked by but not with great ease.

Dawn light flooded the playroom in the loft.
A breeze found an open window and with a waft
Blew into the room its cold morning air,
Announcing to all that morning was here.
At that precise time, Charlie opened the door
And entered the room with purpose for sure.

Unfinished business he had on his mind,
For Spud the hippo he just had to find!
The loft door opening brought a draught so strong
That a book started wobbling, and before very long
It toppled and fell in front of Spud,
Smack on the floor with a very loud 'Thud'!

Charlie raised his eyes and looked up to see
His dear friend sitting there, so patiently.
"Spud!" he exclaimed with a heartfelt cry,
And rushed to his hippo with a tear in his eye.
Hugging him tight and hugging him strong,
He realized Spud had been there all night long.

This huge celebration lasted a while,
And on their faces both had a smile.
At last Charlie took him back where he could be
With all his Ark friends, his close family.
Spud learned a lesson while there on his own:
He'd always been loved and never really alone.

The Present

Charlie awoke, and sat up in bed
And remembered what his mother had said.
What she'd said he found hard to believe:
"It's better to give than to receive."

He thought hard and long – how could this be?
"I'm very happy if there's a present for me.
Would I feel the same if, someday,
I had to give a present away?"

Mum knew best, on her he could rely,
So he said to himself, "I'll give it a try!"
The day was busy for after school
His friend had a party and that was 'cool'!

At the end of the party he asked to take
Away in his pocket some birthday cake.
On the way home this excited little boy
Barely could hide his unbounded joy.

A 'present' he had as a special gift
To give all his animals a little lift.
He'd then be home, safe and sound
To play with them, and be around.

He had cake in his pocket as a surprise
And couldn't wait to see the joy in their eyes.
When he reached home he ran in the door
Then through the hall and across the floor.

To the stairs he rushed, bounding two at a time.
Now at the top, panting after his climb,
He made for the playroom where he knew
That his Ark would be waiting, and his Ark friends too.

Quickly he went to his magical toy,
The excitement consumed this little boy,
And with a deep breath he uttered the spell,
Bringing magic to the ark and animals as well.

He watched the ark's roof lifting off as before
And the animals tumbled out onto the floor.
"Listen everyone, I've got a surprise!"
The animals let out gasps and sighs.

As Charlie pulled out the tissue shape
And began to untie the pretty blue tape,
When he had done, the animals clearly saw
Birthday cake, there, on the loft room floor.

It's hard to describe the joy in the air
In that moment of 'giving' Charlie had there.
The cake was good, which they all ate, it's true,
But the thought that was with this animal crew
Was not the present, but in a special way
Charlie had thought about them all today.

Later that night as Charlie lay in bed,
He remembered what his mother had said.
Smiling, he pulled the duvet up tight
And realised that his mother was right.

Hot and Cold

It was Sunday morning at half past eight.
Charlie was having breakfast and couldn't wait
To go to his animals and play with his toy
For his magical Ark was his special joy.

But there were chores to do to help his mum
To earn pocket money, so he was feeling glum.
But to his delight his mother turned and said,
"Go on, off with you! – I know what's in your head.
You've been good all week and so today
Until lunchtime with your Ark you can play."

Charlie ran to his mother and hugged her so.
After this loving embrace he turned to go,
But his mother said as he reached the door,
"Charlie, 'thank you' is a hug, that's what it's for."
His reply to his mother was merely a smile.
But it meant the world and made life worthwhile.

After cleaning his teeth he ran up the stairs,
Off to the playroom with no worries or cares.
There in the corner was the Ark in its place
Across the room from the large bookcase.

Kneeling before it on the wooden loft floor
He uttered the 'Wordspell' as he'd done before.
"In this ark, right here, right now,
Animals awake, come alive somehow!"
As the lid of the Ark rose into the air
The animals tumbled out in front of him there.
"I can play till lunch!" he said with a shout.
"What shall we play? C'mon, help me out!"

Ben the mouse said, "I haven't a clue!"
Jay made a squeak, Flow gave a moo!
Ace the polar bear thought for a bit
And raised his paw and said, "Got it!"

They watched him closely as he looked at each one.
"We'll play 'Hot and Cold', it's really good fun!
Close your eyes everyone, and no spying!"
Ace then hid his scarf, after untying.

The task now done, Ace said, "Open your eyes!
You must find my scarf, and everyone tries!"
"How can we?" enquired the whale named Spout.
Ace said, "Close to my scarf, a clue I'll give out!

Near, I'll say 'warmer'; if you're nearer, I'll say 'hot'.
'Hotter' if you're closer, 'cold' if you're not!"

The rules now clear in everyone's mind,
They all set off, Ace's scarf for to find.
They searched all over but it couldn't be found
Looked on the windowsill. Looked on the ground.
As the animals looked, Ace was having fun.
He was really glad this game had begun.

"Warmer! Colder! Cold! Warmer! Hot!"
Then Hoff saw something that the others had not.
Around Charlie's neck hung Ace's scarf.
Even Charlie didn't know. Hoff started to laugh.

This made the animals turn and see
The object of their search tied casually
Around their master's neck and shouting as if one,
"It's around your neck Charlie! We all have won!"

Everyone was happy. Ace had lived up to his name.
Charlie hugged them all at the end of their game.
He then said, as he put the animals away,
"That hug was 'thank you' for the fun I've had today!"

As he ran down the stairs he started to laugh:
"How was I to know I was wearing Ace's scarf?"

The Holiday

Early Friday morning and Charlie looked at the time.
The family had to leave by half past nine.
On holiday he was going with his mum and dad,
And whilst he felt happy, he also felt sad.

Although Charlie loved holidays so,
He wasn't sure he wanted to go.
The coast at Brighton waited, but in his mind
He'd have to leave all his Ark friends behind.

The previous day he acted quite glum,
Which was a puzzle for Charlie's mum.
He should be happy. He should be glad.
Instead of which, he looks so sad.

So she gently enquired, "What is it dear?"
"My animals," he said, "I've to leave them here.
Couldn't they all come? They'd be so good!
They'd be no trouble – I promise they would!"

His mother said, "Right Charlie, just for fun
You can't take them all – but you can take one!"
"That's great Mum! Thank you! But who will I choose?
Only one can win, all the others must lose!"

"You must decide, Charlie. You must choose tonight!
And whoever your choice is, you must get it right!"
So all day Thursday he thought hard and long,
A little bit scared that his choice might be wrong.

In the evening he went upstairs as before.
A decision he'd made as he opened the door.
He went to the Ark and uttered the spell,
Bringing life to the Ark and animals as well.

"You can't all come with me, that much is clear.
Mum says I can take one; the rest stay here.
I'm sorry one has to win, the others must lose,
But this is the way I'm going to choose.

Eeny, meeny, miny, moe;
I can't take Pee and I can't take Flo.
One potato, two potato, three potato, four;
You animals are out, so stand by the door!"

Charlie continued in this way
Till two animals were left and had to say,
"Millie and Zeep, it's one of you.
Mum says one; I'd love to take two!

I'll close my eyes and spin around
And point my finger on the ground.
Whoever's the nearest will be the one!"
Charlie spun around and when done
Pointed to Zeep who jumped with delight.
Charlie just knew that his choice had been right.

He picked Zeep up and held him so,
Put the other animals back and turned to go.
He looked at the Ark, and tried not to cry.
Closing the door there was a tear in his eye.

On Friday morning Charlie had to see
Before his holiday his other family,
To say his goodbyes and bid his farewell.
But it was so hard, the truth to tell,
He couldn't look them in the face.
All Charlie could do was sit on his case.

The holiday was good. Charlie and Zeep had fun,
But now they were home, their holiday done.
In the playroom, the Ark was on the floor.
The animals heard Charlie open the door.

The 'Wordspell' was done and eventually
In front of the Ark it was plain to see
That the animals were happy their Master was home!
And never again would they be left all alone.
The animals watched Charlie as they stood by the wall,
And putting Zeep down, he addressed them all.

"I've got you a present. It'll be hard to chew it.
It's rock from Brighton with its name all through it.
It's good to go on holiday, that much is true,
But it's cool to come home and be back with you!"

The Hospital Visit

Hospital was not a place Charlie wanted to go.
Tuesday came, his bag was packed, plans were made, and so
Off he went to have his tonsils out. "Only a little op!"
But of all the places not to go this was at the top.

He didn't want sickness in the op with his throat so very sore,
So he'd had no food and nothing to drink just the night before.
In his bag were Buss and Zeep, a toothbrush and a comb.
In hospital the animals would remind him of his home.

He wanted to take all his Ark friends but mother had said, "No!
You can take these two, Charlie, but the rest of them can't go!"
In the corner of a nice ward he was given a little bed
And very soon had settled in, a light above his head.
On his wrist was a plastic bracelet on which he had his name
And Buss and Zeep had bracelets too – exactly the same.
Mum and Dad were with him – that made him feel at ease,
And the nurses were smiling, kind and anxious to please.
There were pictures on the walls and toys with which to play,
So all in all, Charlie thought, *not a bad place for me to stay*.
The operation went well, and without too much fuss
Charlie was back in his bed along with Zeep and Buss.

He had a slight sore throat and was told to drink a lot
And later to eat ice cream to ease his throat's sore spot.
Now Charlie had to stay in hospital for just one night alone
And then go back the next day, back to his home.

He had a visitor on his only night in and that was his gran.
She'd brought with her a small suitcase, for she had a little plan.

When the nurses weren't looking, she pushed it under his bed.
Charlie smiled broadly and a silent 'thank you' was said.
When everyone had gone, Charlie lay back with a sigh.
He was tired and he was sleepy but a task he had to try.

At the end of the ward a nurse sat working with her light.
It was dark, he had to be careful, she'd be there through the night.
Slowly, carefully and silently Charlie slipped out of his bed
And crawled underneath and pretty soon the 'Wordspell' said.

He opened his gran's suitcase and expecting a surprise,
Gave a gasp as his Ark friends jumped out before his eyes.
They all were there: Ben, Spud, Gray and Red,
Jess, Sam, Splash and Putty underneath his bed.

He played for a while, but the day took its toll.
Soon under the bed and fast asleep was this little soul.
Now the animals had a problem. What were they to do?
Charlie should not be under the bed – this the animals knew.

Gray the owl had a thought and very quickly said,
"C'mon, everyone, we all must help get Charlie back in bed!"
Never was there such a sight that happened on that night:
The activity under the bed as the animals did unite.

They pushed and they pulled and eventually
Hoisted Charlie up to where he should be.
He was back in his bed and tucked up tight.
The animals retreated – the job done right!

In the morning his mum and dad and his gran
Came to visit this little man.

They took him home after a long embrace,
And Gran collected the brown suitcase.

Buss and Zeep went home as well,
And after two days Charlie could tell
That he was better, but he never ever said
Anything about the meeting under his bed.

Snow

In the world of a four-year-old boy,
There's nothing that brings quite as much joy
As seeing when waking up and wanting to go
Out in a landscape covered with snow.

On Thursday evening fell the first snowflake:
Now, deep, crisp and white as Charlie did awake.
He threw back the curtains and with a shout
Cried, "The snow! It's here! I've got to go out!"

He washed, dressed and had breakfast so fast
As though if he didn't, the snow wouldn't last.

He made for the loft to utter the spell,
Gathered up Millie, Ace, and Tex as well,
And turning to go, he heard a loud cough,
So he relented and also picked up Hoff.

Down the stairs he rushed, jumping the last two ,
Grabbed his coat, scarf and Wellingtons too.
Out the door hugging his animals tight,
But had to squint at the bright white light.

His sleigh he soon found and before too long
The animals were quickly being pulled along.
Now the animals had not seen snow before
So could only look and gaze with awe.

What was this world that greeted them now?
And what's this white stuff? It's cold somehow!
Ace was at home for he is a polar bear.
Millie, Hoff and Tex could only stare.

For a while it continued this way
As Charlie pulled them on his sleigh.
Charlie then stopped and said, "All right!
We are all going to have a snowball fight!"

The animals said, "A fight is something we know.
But what's a snowball and what is snow?"

"Just like this!" He threw one at Ace
And the snowball hit him in the face.

Hoff the elephant started to fret:
He'd discovered that snow was cold and wet.
Hoff jumped off the sleigh but to his surprise
He sank in the snow up to his eyes.

Laughing he struggled out. This was good fun,
So soon the snowball fight had begun.
They all enjoyed throwing the snow
Until Charlie decided it was time to go
Back to his home, for he was getting cold.
"Don't stay out too long!" he had been told.

Now home they went indoors, but not before
A snowman they'd built by the front door.
Now warm and snug away from the snow
The animals' faces had a rosy glow.

Charlie had been given a hot chocolate drink.
The animals watched and that made him think.
The drink had warmed him to the core,
So he shared what was left with all four.

Now Charlie and his friends had been out since eight
And having warmed up, they couldn't wait,
So as the clock in the hall chimed half past ten,
Charlie and his animals went out again.

They went out six times during this day,
Laughed a lot and enjoyed their play.
They would never forget and did now know
All about snowballs, fights and snow.

The Tidy-Up

Charlie's mother said, "I have to confess
Your playroom, Charlie, is in a bit of a mess.

So before you can go out today
Tidy your playroom before you play."
Charlie's heart sank. He knew she was right.
Toys and books everywhere – a messy sight.

He would have to set to and tidy the place.
If he left it alone it would be a disgrace.
Help he would seek. He knew where to go:
He'd ask his Ark friends, Buss, Pee and Flo.

So cheered by this thought, he went up the stairs
And made for the playroom with no worries or cares.
Charlie said the 'Wordspell' as he'd done before,
Watched as his animals tumbled onto the floor.

Out of the Ark they came: Flo, Buss and Pee,
Emm, Spud, Splash, Zeep, Spout and Gee.
Soon all were there, huddled in a group,
Looking up in wonder was this little troupe.

Charlie addressed them and raising his voice,
"We've got to tidy up. We have no choice!"
As he spoke there was a tremor in his lip.
"There's stuff everywhere! Mum says it's a tip!

If we all help and tidy it up today,
Mum says that I can go out and play!"
Hayes the pig said, "It isn't a sight.
I like stuff everywhere. I think it's all right!"

Charlie and the others let out a moan,
And it was clear that Hayes was on his own.
Each animal was given a job to do,
And very soon they all set to.

Books were collected. Some large, some small.
Arranged in size both short and tall.
The animals stood in a line and formed a chain,
Passed books to each other time and again

And after a few minutes they had a smile on their face.
For the books were back in the large bookcase.
Then they started on the toys and shoes,
Papers and crayons – no time to lose.

Pencils were put back in their box,
A couple of vests, a couple of socks.
Charlie and the animals picked up the pace:
Before you could blink things were back in their place.

Working as a team, everyone could see
The results of their efforts quite clearly.
Hayes the pig said as he stood by the door,
"I preferred it the way the room was before"

The animals laughed and Charlie did too.
Only Hayes didn't laugh. He hadn't a clue.
Gray the owl said, "One piece of advice.
I'll say it just once. I won't say it twice.

Take care of your things, Charlie, and you'll find
That you'll have a tidy room and a tidy mind."
Charlie then said, "Every one of you is a star!
Thanks for helping me and being the friends you are."

In the playroom, in the Ark, the animals had to stay,
But for Charlie, now he could go out and play.

The Garden Adventure

"Oh please, Mum. Couldn't we try?"
Charlie let out a heartfelt sigh.
"My Ark's in the playroom. It's always there.
If in the garden, we'd get lots of air.
You could carry it down. I know you could.
If you did I promise I'd be ever so good."

"Enough now, Charlie," his mother said.
"I'll do it for you. You're hurting my head!"
In no time at all Mother had done the task.
Charlie knew he'd only have to ask.
The Ark now on the grass under a large oak tree,
Charlie looked around to check no one could see,

Spoke his magic 'Wordspell' soft and slow
And saw in the Ark a magical glow.
The lid of the Ark rose into the air.
In front of Charlie the animals stood there.

Now they were surprised at where they stood
Whatever it was it wasn't brown wood.

The ground underfoot felt springy and soft
And different somehow to the floor in the loft.
"It's called grass." said Charlie. "It grows and it's green."
All the animals murmured – grass they'd never seen.
Around the 'grass' there were bushes and trees.
Charlie explained this to put them at ease.

Spout enquired, "What's that in the sun?"
Charlie said, "A birdbath! C'mon, let's have fun!"
They all ran over to it and looked up in awe.
"It's a bath for birds," said Charlie. "That's what it's for."

Spout the whale said, " I do miss the sea!"
And Splash the dolphin said with glee,
"We could get in the water and pretend
That we are at sea once more again!"

"Good idea!" said Charlie. "C'mon, up you pop!"
And quickly placed Splash and Spout on the top.
They stared at the water and shouting "Wheeee!"
Both threw themselves in immediately.

For a minute or two they both had fun,
Splashing in the birdbath there in the sun.
Then something happened which set them thinking.
For Splash and Spout started sinking.

They were only soft toy animals, you see,
And never had really been in the sea.
Water had made them heavy, of that there's no doubt,
And so they both shouted, "Help! Get us out!"
Charlie and the other animals saw their distress.
Charlie said, " C'mon! Let's help them out of this mess!"

He lifted onto the birdbath Spud and Buss,
And they began the rescue without any fuss.
They grabbed Splash and they grabbed Spout
And slowly they gradually pulled them out.
Charlie then helped all of them down.
Spout said, "We were lucky not to drown!"

Splash didn't say anything. He was too upset.
He wanted to swim but not to get wet!
Charlie then said, "Please try not to cry,
We've got to find a way to get you both dry!"
Later Charlie's mother, at the end of the day,
Went into the garden to put the Ark away.

What she saw made her stop, blink and then smile.
A sight greeted her, which would last quite a while:
Dangling and dripping in the bright sunshine
Were Splash and Spout on the washing line.

Why were they there? On this thought she did dwell.
But we know, don't we? But we'll never ever tell.

The Bear's Smile

Five o'clock and evening was here.
The dark and wet outside provided little cheer.
Charlie stood by the playroom door
And heard a voice he couldn't ignore.

The voice was soft and came to him there
From a little girl with bunches on the third stair.
"You're off to your Ark friends, aren't you?
I don't suppose I could come too?"

I don't think I've mentioned this before,
But Charlie has a sister. She's only four.
Her name is Sally and she's a joy to know,
Can't keep still and always on the go.

Charlie looks after her whenever he can,
And if she needs him he's always at hand.
She doesn't play with Charlie's animals too much,
In fact Charlie often tells her, "Please don't touch!"

She has her teddy and he will do.
It sticks with her just like glue.
She's never without it. It's always there.
Charlie has his animals. She has her bear.

"Okay, you can come, but wait here for a mo,
And when I shout 'ready', in you can go!"
Charlie went into the playroom and closed the door.
Sally stood outside with her bear on the floor.

She was curious and listened and kept so still
But couldn't hear a thing – that is, until
Charlie opened the door and with a furrowed brow
Said, "C'mon Sal, you can come in now!"
(Charlie had said the 'Wordspell' while on his own:
He can only do this when he is alone!)

She entered the playroom and could only stare
At all the Ark animals sitting there.
Charlie introduced them all one by one,
Which took a time, and when he was done
Enquired of Sally, "What shall we do?"
To which Sally replied, "Have a party for you!

We could get it all ready at least by six
And have lemonade and large choccy bics!"
Charlie said, "Yes, and have jelly too!
And ice cream as well! Well done you!"

Filled with excitement, they ran across the floor,
Out of the room and slammed the door.
The bang made the animals jump in the air
And after settling they saw… Sally's bear.

Now this was unusual for this little troupe
To find in their number, a stranger in their group.
"What is your name?" asked the whale called Spout
But Sally's bear just sat and said nowt.

For what seemed an age they tried and they tried
To talk to the bear, which was silent, then cried.
The animals all asked, "What's upset you so?
And why do you cry. We're your friends, you know!"

The bear said, "I cry 'cos I don't have a name!"
The animals agreed that this was a shame.
"But you're Sally's Bear!" Ben said in a shout,
"And that's a good name, of that there's no doubt!"

All agreed that name right there and then
And 'Sally's Bear' thanked little mouse Ben.
When Charlie and Sally returned with the tea,
Sally's Bear had a smile for all to see.
The children wondered what had taken place.
But we know why there's a smile on his face.

One For Now, One For Later

It was not a good day. Charlie felt very glum.
His gran had been taken ill, according to his mum.
Together they would visit her. That was his mother's plan.
"Right," his mother said. "Get ready as fast as you can!"

He loved his gran and he hated to feel
That she was in bed, alone and ill.
She told him stories and made him laugh.
He recalled the one about Emm the giraffe.

He would do his best to make her well,
Although what he could do, he could not tell.
Shortly they both were on their way in the car
To go to the hospital. It wasn't too far.

Charlie had with him a large bin sack
On the seat beside him, as he sat in the back.
There were bulges and lumps and he nursed it quite tight,
For his plan, if it worked, would make Gran alright.

Soon they arrived to see Gran in bed
Propped up on pillows, and 'hellos' were said.
They spoke for a while and it was good to see
Gran's spirits were high. She talked happily.

Then Charlie's mother was called to the phone
Leaving Charlie and his gran for a minute alone.
Charlie said as he reached down into his sack,
"I've a surprise for you but I want them back!

Now close your eyes, and please don't peep!"
And produced Spud the hippo and Jess the sheep.
Gran opened her eyes, her heart full of joy,
Seeing the 'gift' from this little boy.

"Every day, every visit, there will be
Different animals for you to see.
They'll stay all day and stay all night
Until you're better and completely all right!"

"Thank you Charlie, It's a wonderful thought.
I'm really touched by what you've brought."

She kissed him on his cheek and then his forehead
And smiling sweetly she gently said,
"One for now, and one for later, please remember this.
Everyone needs affection. Everyone needs a kiss."
Charlie met her eyes and gave a knowing smile
And turning he left her room so she could rest a while.

Every day for two weeks Charlie kept his word
And then something quite remarkable occurred.
Gran was suddenly better. Charlie jumped for joy.
It was the 'bestest news ever' for this little boy.

They took Gran home and settled her in
And Charlie approached her and said with a grin,
"I'm bursting with something I have to tell.
I'm so glad you're better, I'm so glad you're well.

My animals are happy and I am too.
Their company in hospital saw you through."
So saying he reached forward and gave her a kiss.
Smiling he said, "I must tell you this,
One for now and one for later, it's what you said,
I remembered it didn't I?" – a tear was shed.

Those words, thought Charlie, *I'll never forget.*
And neither will you, I'm willing to bet!

The Question

A question I am often asked and now I will impart
Is how Charlie got his Ark and how it all did start.
To answer this, I must take you back to many years ago,
When Charlie's gran was a little girl of four or five or so.

She had no brothers or sisters with whom she could play
So played, on her own, with her animals every day.
Her other toys were mostly dollies, but none gave her the joy
As the animals that her father had had when he was just a boy.

She looked a lot like Sally does, with bunches in her hair.
Whenever she needed anything, her father would be there.
He loved his daughter dearly, this was plain to see.
Nothing was too much trouble if it filled her life with glee.

A carpenter, by trade, his living was made with wood,
And if I do say so myself, his work was rather good.
He could make anything – anything you could think of.
The detail was incredible, crafted with care and love.

So when his daughter told him of her strange request,
He smiled and he winked and said he'd do his best.
She'd asked him to build an Ark, but not so much a boat:
A small one for her animals that wouldn't need to float.

"Why an Ark?" her father asked directly to her face
"An Ark for all my animals seems the natural place!"
In moments like these a father knows the sign.
There's no point in debating. It only wastes the time.

So early the very next day, he started choosing wood.
He wanted to make it magical, if he possibly could.
Only the best would do. He found some beautiful pine,
Elm, beech, maple and hickory: that would do just fine.

Mahogany for the roof and then some old wood glue.
This would be his gift to her. Maybe future generations too.
So around his other chores he worked both day and night.
It was a labour of love and it had to be just right.

One morning after the rain he entered his old workshop.
What he saw made him blink and also made him stop.

The Ark was on his workbench – that was no surprise,
But something happened, for the sight that met his eyes
Was a rainbow shining in the Ark, sparkling oh so bright,
Shimmering magically in the early morning light.
It took his breath away. How could this possibly be?
What had made the wonderful colours he could see?

His eyes settled on an old chisel that lay in the awakening sun,
Which poured through the window as the day had just begun.
The blade of the tool reflected the light beams towards the Ark,
Which gave the illusion of rainbow colours shining in the dark.

A logical explanation of that there was no doubt,
But it gave him reason to pause having worked it out.
This Ark was magical! There was something special here.
A feeling he could almost touch. On his cheek a tear.

He'd finish it today, there was nothing else for it,
Give it tomorrow and he knew she would adore it.
When she received it she felt so glad,
Words were beyond her. She hugged her dad.

They stood there hugging in a fond embrace,
Sheer delight etched on her face.
His talent had crafted a gift of love,
Blessed by a rainbow as if from above.

Now an old lady, she remembered that day
When given the Ark with which to play,
So it seemed right to give her grandson then
Her blessed toy to play with again.

Her smile to Charlie tells him she knows
That the Ark is special when the magic shows.
For the animals come to life in the blink of an eye,
Just as they did back in those years gone by.

The Decoration

This story involves Robert and for that I'm glad
For until now, I haven't really mentioned Charlie's dad.
Robert loves his children deeply and is a gentle man,
And Robert's mother is of course little Charlie's gran.

He has his own decorating business and that is fine,
For it keeps him very busy for most of the time.
So when Charlie asked him in a very special way,
"Please Dad, can you decorate the playroom in which I play?"

He thought for a minute and said with a grin,
"I've got a lot on, but I'll try and fit it in!"
"Thanks!" said Charlie. "My walls – they're painted white,
And a little bit grubby – they look quite a sight!"
His dad said, "I know exactly what you mean.
The room will be better, if it's nice and clean!
I'll make a list of the things that I need to use;
Just let me know the colours you would like to choose.

I'll get the paint in a day or two
And decorate your room for you!"
Charlie hugged his dad, but then he had to go
To his animals in the Ark, so he could let them know.

He entered the playroom, a smile on his face
And approached the Ark in the corner – its usual place.
He whispered the 'Wordspell' as he'd done before
And watched as the animals tumbled onto the floor.

"I've got some news!" he said. "It's really great!
It's our playroom – Dad's going to decorate!"
The animals were excited. Ben the mouse jumped for joy!
He loved hearing news like this from this little boy.

"I've got to choose the colours – you can help me too!
What would you all like? Just give me your view!"
Charlie watched as the animals formed a little group.
Decisions were always done this way with this special troupe.

After a while Gray the owl approached Charlie and said,
"We need five colours, but they don't include red!
We've written this list, please give it to your dad.
If he buys these, we know we'll all be glad!"

Charlie thanked them, for he knew that Gray was wise,
Rushed out of the room to give his dad the surprise.
His father looked at the list, and phoned his local store:
"I'll get these for you, Charlie, but heaven knows what for!"

Two days later, five pots of paint and brushes were waiting
By the Ark in the playroom, ready for painting.
Charlie's father was to start that very same night
To decorate the room, to make it fresh and bright.

Charlie and the animals could only look and stare
At the paint and the brushes lying there.
Gray the owl spoke, saying, "C'mon, you crew!"
And in the time it takes to blush, they all set to.

The tins of paint were opened and the brushes dipped in quick.
The animals started painting, but Hoff the elephant had a trick.
He filled his trunk with paint and then he just had to say,
"Watch this you lot!" and the paint he started to spray!

At this rate the painting was fast and was fun.
At the end they all stood back and admired what they'd done.
There was purple, pink, blue, yellow and green;
Behind the Ark on the wall a rainbow could be seen.

Charlie and the animals were pleased. Their plan had worked well,
Although what Charlie's father would say, they really couldn't tell.
When he entered the playroom later that night
He was greeted by a rainbow, gleaming and shining bright.
How had this happened? This rainbow was certainly clever!
But it's our secret, isn't it? For ever and ever and ever!

Starry Night

Friday evening and Charlie was tucked up tight,
Snuggled in his bed like he was every night.
The animals took their turn to be with him whilst he slept.
Tonight was Putty's turn and when he knew, he leapt
Straight into Charlie's arms and gave him the biggest hug.
Now, lying there, they were warm, cosy and snug.

When Charlie's head touched the pillow he went out like a light.
It had been a busy day for this little mite.
He had been so very tired but didn't want to show it,
He didn't even want his mum and dad to know it.
Taking care of Charlie whilst he slept was Putty's favourite task.
All the animals felt the same. All Charlie did was ask.

Putty loved the night and the stillness that came,
So sleeping through the night seemed such a shame.
He loved all the stars when they glittered and shone
And was sad when they blinked and were suddenly gone.
He loved the airplanes' red lights as they went to and fro,
Taking people to places they wanted to go.

He loved the sounds of the night. The wind in the trees,
Owls hooting, foxes playing and the rustle of the leaves.
As Putty was thinking about all he was thankful for,
Charlie stirred and his pillow fell on the floor.
This woke the little fellow up and he gave a little moan,
So Putty held his hand to tell him he wasn't alone.
Charlie was afraid of the dark and also of the night.
Putty said, "Don't worry! Everything's all right!
I want to tell you now what's in the sky above,
I want to share with you all the things I love!"
And before another word was said,
Both had wriggled down to the end of Charlie's bed.

Looking out the window, Putty said, "Listen to me,
Look up into the sky and tell me what you see."
"Oh! I see a beautiful star!" Charlie said with a sigh.
"Stars are the nightlights that brighten up the sky."
As soon as Putty said this, a large cloud drifted by.
Charlie's star was gone and he didn't know why.

"Oh no!" said Charlie. "My star has gone away
Will it come back and stay another day?"

Putty replied, "Listen, tell me what you hear!"
"Nothing," said Charlie, in his eye a tear.
"See what happens now, and watch with care."
The cloud passed by as Charlie did stare:
His star was back in exactly the same place.
You should have seen the smile on his face!

Suddenly the sky was filled with stars so bright,
All twinkling and shining, an amazing sight.
"They're lovely," said Charlie. "What a lot there are!"
"Yes!" said Putty. "And your guiding star
Was shown to you first, so you knew where to look,
Before you saw the others with the second look you took."

Charlie asked, "Will I find my star again? – Where should I start?"
Putty replied, "You will feel it in your heart!
Welcome to night school, Charlie. Never be afraid.
Your guiding star will always come to your aid.
Take a deep breath and never have fear.
Feel the light and love that is always here.

You too can shine, you know it's true,
Just like the stars, by just being you."
Charlie felt happy and climbed back into bed,
Knowing that not another word would be said.
Putty kissed Charlie goodnight as he closed his little eyes,
And in his dreams he celebrated the beauty of the skies.

The Unlucky Day

Early morning, cuddled up in his duvet, Charlie knew it was here.
It had arrived! The day he'd been dreading all year.
It was a Friday, and with the weekend coming, normally a good day.
But today was the 'thirteenth' and was 'unlucky', some would say.

With Charlie in his bed was Spud the hippo, and both kept so still,
For they were happy in the warm and didn't want to move, until
Charlie's mother gave an early morning shout!
"It's time you got up Charlie – I've got to go out!

Sally is already dressed and has had her breakfast too,
So please get up and be quick, or I don't know what I'll do!"
Charlie slowly got up, went into the bathroom with Spud in tow,
Turned the sink tap on, and watched as the water did flow.

It rushed into the sink, faster than normal, which was a big surprise
For it started splashing everywhere and into Charlie's eyes.
His pyjamas were soaking and Spud was also wet.
Spud said, "Today is unlucky and it hasn't started yet!"

They mopped up all the water. Charlie quickly washed his face,
Ran back into his bedroom and having picked up the pace,
Tried to dress quickly, but his jumper just couldn't be found.
Then he saw it, put it on, but alas the wrong way round.

The back was at the front. Spud laughed and started to giggle.
He pointed it out to Charlie, and after a chuckle and a wriggle,
Charlie put it on again, this time the correct way,
Saying, "I've got a feeling I'm not going to like today!"

Now at breakfast, Charlie had some honey on his bread,
Spud sat on one side, Sally on the other, and Sally then said,
"Friday the thirteenth is lucky for me! – I really have no fear!"
"It's not for me!" said Charlie. "I wish it wasn't here!"

As he said this he accidently knocked his bread onto the floor
And noticed to his horror that the honey had started to pour
All over the floor tiles, for the honey side was down.
"No!" shouted Charlie. His mother gave him a frown.

"That's enough of that! Do calm down! All right?"
"Sorry, Mum!" said Charlie, "I'm getting a bit uptight!"
He picked up the bread and honey and quickly mopped it up.
Then gave a long, drawn-out sigh as he drained his special cup.

Charlie's mother then said, "Right, we've got to go!
The shopping that I need won't do it itself, you know.
You can bring Spud along, Charlie – and Sally, remember, do,
You're staying with a friend tonight so I'll drop you off too!"

Before you could say the word 'shop' they all were on their way
Charlie held Spud and wondered what else would happen today.
Sally was 'dropped off' and to the supermarket they did drive.
Charlie held Spud tightly and very soon they did arrive.

They parked the car and as they walked to the store,
Charlie avoided the cracks in the car park – just to make sure
That nothing else happened to him, for today was really scary.
I'm not touching anything, he thought, *because I'm wary!*

Charlie's mother fetched a trolley and started to do her shop.
Lots of things were put in the trolley and Charlie then said, "Stop!
"Look – there's my favourite cereal with nuts, raisins and wheat.
Please can I have some – It would make a lovely treat!"

"All right!' said Charlie's mother. "Go on, but take just one!"
Charlie, still holding onto Spud, to the cereals did run.
Now the boxes of this cereal were piled really high
In a pyramid display to catch the customers' eye.

Charlie didn't think and grabbed the nearest one.
Spud exclaimed, "Oh, Oh!" for he saw what had been done.
The cereal boxes started wobbling and, what's more,
Crashed down heavily onto the supermarket floor.

Charlie stared in horror at the boxes everywhere.
A member of staff quickly came. All Charlie could do was stare.
"I'm so sorry!" said Charlie. "I grabbed one in a hurry!"
"Accidents will happen," said the man, "Please don't worry!"

Charlie whispered to Spud, "It's an unlucky day. It's what I said."
Spud turned to Charlie, saying, "I wish we'd stayed in bed!"
Soon Spud, Charlie and his mother continued with their shop.
Now at the checkout, Charlie saw something that made him stop.

On the floor by the till was a little leather purse of brown,
So Charlie went over to it, and bending down,
Picked it up, looked at it, and saw how much it cost,
And he realised that it must have been accidently lost.

He immediately handed it over to the girl at the till.
"Oh what a relief!" said the girl. "That nice old lady called Jill
Lost her purse earlier. There's a reward for it being found!
Where did you find it?" Charlie pointed to the ground.

Later, as Charlie sat in the car with his best friend near,
He held some money tightly and had a grin from ear to ear.
Charlie whispered to Spud, "It's not such an unlucky day,
'Cos each day is what you make of it, or so my mum would say!"

A Story for Hoff

"Bless you!" said Charlie hearing a loud sneeze from Hoff.
"Thank you!" said the elephant. "I've a cold and a cough!"
"I need to take great care of you," Charlie then said.
"I think I'd better pick you up and put you in my bed!"

At this suggestion Hoff's face was a picture of delight.
He knew Charlie would take care of him and he would be all right.
Charlie had been playing with his Ark friends for most of the day.
The hours pass so quickly when he spends his time this way.

He hadn't really been aware that Hoff was a little ill.
He was having fun with Zeep and Putty, that is, and was until
Hoff's sneeze had made everyone jump in the air with fright.
Large elephants sneeze loudly, a fact that Hoff proved right!

Charlie scooped Hoff up into his arms and as he turned to go,
Thought he'd give Hoff company and chose the cow called Flo.
Minutes later Hoff was tucked up tight in Charlie's little bed.
Flo the cow sat on the pillow inches from his head.

Charlie sat at the foot of the bed
And turning to Hoff he gently said,
"Would you like a story to make the time go by?"
"I'd like that!" said Hoff sadly with a heartfelt sigh.

"Something to take my mind of this cold and my runny nose!"
So this is the story that little Charlie chose.
"Once upon a time," said Charlie, "the animals tell of a tale
All about a dolphin, a shark and a big blue whale.

Now the fish in the seas were frightened to swim
For fear of the shark who was big and was grim.
They stayed under rocks on the bed of the sea
And never did swim, in case they did see
The evil, nasty shark, for he would
Have them for breakfast if he could.

But there was a dolphin who had no fear
And helped his fish friends if they were near.

He'd swim around and have a look to see
If the shark was anyway near in the sea,
And if the coast was clear he'd bob about
So the fish would know it was safe to come out.

But the shark was cunning and had a plan,
Thinking, "I'll eat those fishes if I can!"
He closed his eyes as if he was asleep.
One eye was closed but the other risked a peep!

He saw the dolphin do his usual stuff,
Then the fish came out, and he knew his bluff
Had worked. On his face was a smile:
He'd have a big breakfast in a little while!

But a big blue whale was passing by
And saw the shark's twitching eye.
He knew the shark was feigning sleeping
While really awake and keeping peeping.
So he swam up behind the shark, this whale of blue,
And in his loudest voice he shouted, "Boooo!"

The shark jumped and shivered with fright
And swam away fast, out of sight!
On the big blue whale's face was a happy grin,
For he knew the shark wouldn't be seen again.

So the moral of this story is simple but true:
You might think you're big but there's bigger than you.
You might have a plan but it's doomed to fail,
For behind you just might be a big blue whale!"

Charlie finished his story and closed his book.
Hoff and Flo were asleep, he knew from their look,
And in their dreams they dreamt of a tale
Of a dolphin, a shark and a big blue whale.

The Special Birthday

Charlie had been awake for quite a little while.
He'd thought of a plan, and this plan had made him smile.
Six o'clock in the morning and the bright dazzling sun
Streamed through his bedroom window – the day had begun.

Outside, the birds were singing their every-morning tune;
He'd a lot to do today, better get started – and soon!

He jumped out of bed, went to the bathroom and dressed,
Quickly had his breakfast, and no one would have guessed
What was in his mind as he made the last cornflake disappear.
He was excited about this event, for he'd waited nearly a year.

Tomorrow was his mother's birthday – a really special day.
He and his animal friends would ensure it stayed that way.
After cleaning his teeth he went to the playroom, where he knew
His Ark would be waiting and his animals too.

The magic 'Wordspell' was very quickly said,
And soon the animals knew what was in his head.
"It's Mum's birthday tomorrow, and I have a plan!
We've got to make letters just as fast as we can!

They've got to be really big, and we can colour them too.
I've got my crayons with me. I've yellow, red and blue,
Orange, purple, pink, brown and green:
Being big and colourful, they'll be easily seen.

I've also got some scissors, paper and some string,
So will you all help me and do this special thing?"
Before you could say 'Ark' they all had started work,
Worked really hard and none of them did shirk.

Buss the lion and the horse called Gee
Cut out the letters and said with glee,
"They're ready for colouring – Please take care!"
Pee the dog and Jess the sheep were very soon there.

They collected the letters and the string as well,
And after an hour, as far as they could tell,
Their job was finished, and all were so glad
That they had assisted in helping this lad.

All the letters were attached to the string
By sticky tape, to help them cling.
Charlie then said, "Thanks, but we're not finished yet!
We'll keep them for tomorrow and mustn't forget!"

The next day Charlie and his animal crew
Knew exactly what they had to do.
To the top two bedrooms they went in the house,
Creeping slowly, silently and quiet as a mouse.

With Gray the owl's help, string was strung just right
From bedroom window on the left to bedroom window on the right.
In no time at all the rest of the job was done.
"Thank you!" Charlie said. "Well done, everyone!"

Charlie was pleased. On his face he had a beam;
He really couldn't have done it without his special team.
When Charlie's mother returned from doing her afternoon shop,
She entered her garden and then had to stop.

Twenty-four letters, gleaming, did gently swing,
Hanging across the windows of the house on string.
The large letters shone brightly and in plain view
Spelt: "Happy Birthday Mum – I Love You!"

Had Charlie done this? It was certainly done well.
But we know don't we, but we couldn't ever tell!

Many Hearts and Much Love

In the garden Saturday and Charlie was cross. Sally was too.
They'd had 'words', as a brother and sister sometimes do.
It was over nothing at all and both were upset.
Funny how careless words are difficult to forget.

Charlie regretted what he had somehow said.
He knew Sally was crying whilst lying on her bed.
This upset Charlie. He loved his sister dearly.
He'd have to make it up to her and do it soon – clearly!

He then let out a heartfelt sigh
And slowly raised his eyes to the sky,
Then, waving his arms all about,
He let out this pleading shout.

"How I do it – I really don't care!
But all I want is to put love in the air!"
Now when a wish is spoken direct from the heart,
It is carried on the breeze and magical things start.

Now Charlie's little wish was carried up into the air
And somehow through a window that was open there.
Sitting on Charlie's bed was the dog called Pee.
All the previous night he'd been with Charlie, you see.

Now the little dog's face when he heard his master's voice
Was a picture, for he realised that he had no choice.
He had to tell his Ark friends, of that there was no doubt.
Gray the owl was wise, so somehow they'd work it out.

Later Charlie returned Pee the dog to the Ark.
Pee waited till Charlie had gone before saying, "Hark!
I've got something to say. All of you listen to me!"
He then told the animals of their master's little plea.
Gray the owl then said, "Love in the air – Ummmm!
We can't have Charlie feeling a little glum!

I've thought of a plan – if we can carry it through,
Our little master will be far from blue."
He then put his wing to his beak
And then very softly did he speak.
"Mark my words carefully and well!" he said.
"We need paper, scissors and crayons of red!"

The animals rushed around and collected what Gray did ask.
And it wasn't very long before they had completed their task.
Gray the owl then said, "There's something I must impart.
Colour the paper red and on each piece draw a heart!"
All the animals got busy. You couldn't believe what you saw –
Hearts were drawn on red paper all over the floor.

Gray then said, " Right – we've got to cut these hearts out!
Spud! – you look out for Charlie. If he comes – Shout!
When they are cut out, collect them as fast as you can
And then bring them to me. Here is my little plan!"
Now the rest of what was said, I really couldn't tell,
But trust me – stories of Charlie's Ark always turn out well.

A little while later, a sad Charlie returned to the Ark to play.
All the animals were there and Gray did then say,
"Charlie, earlier today we heard your little plea.
Take this gift in both hands, and carefully listen to me.
Don't look at what is given but throw it into the air,
And your wish will be truly granted. This I swear!"

Why Charlie should do this he hadn't a clue,
But straight away he did what he'd been asked to do.
Dozens of red paper hearts fluttered all around,
Dazzling and shimmering before settling on the ground.

The sight was amazing and drew gasps from everyone there.
Charlie's wish was granted. He now had love in the air.
Every one of the animals had a hug and an embrace.
Charlie's frown was gone and there was a smile upon his face.

They collected all the hearts up as quick as could be
And Charlie ran to get Sally so she could share his glee.
When Sally arrived, she did what Charlie had done,
A smile on her face too – all were having fun.

Their 'words' were now a thing of the past,
For little disagreements must never really last.
Charlie said, "Sorry Sal! – I didn't mean to hurt you!"
Sally said, "I was as much to blame – I'm so sorry too!"

Many times the hearts were thrown landing on the floor.
Laughing, playing, brother and sister were friends again once more.
It's only a small word, but in a very peculiar way
'Sorry' shouldn't ever be the hardest word to say.

The Lightning Tree

Charlie sighed. The day had been long.
But the air was heavy. Something was wrong.
He looked out the window. The sky was pink.
Gray the owl was beside him and gave him a wink.

"I've seen this before," he said, frowning a lot.
"There's a big storm brewing and it's going to be hot!"
"How can a storm be hot?" Charlie asked his friend.
"Well, there'll be thunder, lightning and rain without end.

Before then, it'll be warm and close," said Gray.
"The birds will stop singing and hide away.
As the storm moves closer, a breeze it will send,
And the hairs on your neck will stand up on end."

"Oh dear!" said Charlie. "That does sound bad!"
"Don't worry, Charlie, please don't be sad.
The storm will pass and will not stay,
For tomorrow is another day."

They watched out the window as clouds passed by,
Marvelling at the colours in the troubled sky.
Then, pointing, Charlie said, "Gray, please tell me,
Why do they call that 'The Lightning Tree'?"

"There's a story to that, my faithful friend:
That tree is proud and will not bend.
It's taller than all the others around.
A taller tree could not be found.

That oak tree has stood for lots of years,
Witnessed many joys, witnessed many tears.
Five years ago, in a storm such as this,
Lightning struck it and gave it its kiss.

It changed the tree's shape and did create
An image of a fork you would find by your plate.
The people around here would not take it down,
And now it's a feature of this little town.

With this coming storm, you will see
Lightning strike this lightning tree."
Gray and Charlie watched in wonder
As the storm came close with its thunder.

Gray said, "There's an old story I know:
We watch for lightning to make its show.
Then we count slowly, and you will see
The number we get to, we divide by three.
That will tell us, and tell us clear,
How many miles the storm's from here."

So they both started to count in time
With asides that seemed to rhyme.

"ONE – The counting's begun…

TWO – This should be fun.

THREE – The suspense is killing…

FOUR – But the excitement is thrilling.

FIVE – We can't wait to know…

SIX – When the thunder will start to go."

A moaning, rumbling, threatening sound
Invaded the air, the house, the ground.
"Six divided by three is two!" Gray said.
"It's two miles away! Hang on to the bed!"
Charlie was so excited he could not speak.
This was the best thing that had happened all week.

But just as Charlie was thinking this,
Lightning struck, gave the tree its kiss.
Charlie jumped, and all he could see
Was this tall oak lit up like a Christmas tree.

It was silhouetted against the dark purple sky.
And looked so awesome Charlie did sigh.
There was something magical in the air right now.
They both could feel it, and Charlie said, "Wow!"

In a few minutes the storm had passed.
Storms like these never really last.
Charlie snuggled down in bed along with Gray,
His mind filled with the thoughts of today.

He thought of the tree, the storm and the rain,
The thunder and lightning, and fell asleep once again.

Bad Dreams – Good Friends

A few years ago Charlie had bad dreams, which just wasn't right,
For they often turned into nightmares nearly every night.
Although Putty the monkey kept him company most of the time,
He felt helpless. They occurred without reason or rhyme.

Charlie would toss around in his bed, his eyes closed tight.
It was like he had a fever and been given a bad fright.
Putty decided to do something. What on earth could he do?
He would speak to Gray the wise owl and the rest of the crew.

Putty sat and watched Charlie moaning as he lay,
Till morning came and the nightmares would go away.
Putty snuggled as close as he could possibly get,
To comfort and love him so he didn't fret.

Time passed and now seven o'clock, Charlie opened his eyes.
"Morning Charlie!" said Putty. "It's time for you to rise!"
Charlie forced a grin and gave his friend a hug.
"A new day!" said Putty. Charlie just gave a shrug.

Putty said, "C'mon, we've got things to do!
I need to speak with the gang from the Ark about you!"
Charlie then asked, "What about me?"
Putty replied, "Just wait and see!"

At breakfast Putty watched Charlie. Not his normal self now:
He was quiet, withdrawn and hid a concerned scowl.
Putty had to talk with Gray and the animal crew.
Surely there was something he and the rest could do.

Back at the Ark later, Putty was with the animal crowd.
Worried animals gathered around. Putty spoke loud.
"Charlie is having very bad dreams which have to cease!
Gray, you're the wise one here, how can Charlie get peace?"

Gray thought for a moment and then he said…
"There's something we must do before he goes to bed.
We must make him laugh, giggle and smile
And banish the bad thoughts just for a while.

This must be our aim. This must be our task,
So when he shuts his eyes, the happiness will last!"
The Ark animals agreed this was a good plan.
"Can we do it? – Yes! We can!"

While Charlie was at school, the animals worked hard.
They used paint, crayons and chalk on pieces of card.
All were cut out in various shapes and sizes:
This would be one of the greatest surprises.

There were beards, moustaches, glasses and a bow tie,
False noses, false chins and patches for the eye.
At last their task was done. Charlie would soon be back.
Their many creations were put in a sack.

It was taken to Charlie's bedroom and put under his bed.
They knew what to do. Not a single word was said.
The animals then hid under the bed, save Putty who gave a hop
And snuggled down with Charlie's pillow right on the top.

They then waited for their master to come up to sleep.
The excitement grew, there were giggles, some risked a peep!
Charlie went into the bathroom to do his teeth and wash.
The animals listened to the "splish" and the "splosh!"

Charlie went to his bed and slowly climbed in.
He cuddled Putty fondly when he saw him.
Putty then said, "Charlie, please close your eyes!"
The next thing Charlie heard was: "Surprise!"

Charlie opened his eyes to such a funny sight.
He couldn't believe what he saw on that night.

All the animals were dressed up with many disguises,
Moustaches, glasses, wigs – so many surprises.
They danced around, posing with a wiggle.
Charlie couldn't help himself – he started to giggle.

Now laughing is catching, so when Charlie laughed,
So did the animals, for they all looked quite daft.
The fun and laughter was good to see.
Charlie settled down quite happily.

The animals were so pleased. Gray's plan was good.
Charlie had reacted exactly how he should.
There was a smile on his face as he closed his eyes.
No nightmares tonight. Just love in the skies!

Charlie's Christmas Eve

Eleven o'clock on Christmas Eve, and Charlie couldn't sleep.
He was excited and wide-awake, with no thoughts of counting sheep.
Santa was coming tonight with presents, if he'd been good.
He tried to remember if he'd done the things he should.

"Yes," he thought. "Mum said I've been a good boy,
So Santa should be bringing me at least one good toy."
Outside, sparkling, glistening snowflakes, zigzagging, fell and lay,
Bringing carpets and cloaks of white to make a special Christmas Day.

It was Millie the panda's turn to be with him tonight in bed,
And she was so happy when she heard her name being said.
"It's Millie tonight!" Charlie announced and she had to jump for joy.
She'd been picked to spend Christmas Eve with this little boy.

The animals, although disappointed, were glad for Millie
They couldn't all sleep with Charlie. That would be silly!
Charlie and Millie chatted about the day to come.
His Gran was coming over to stay with Dad and Mum.

They could all go in the snow and have a wonderful day,
And if Gran was careful, might go on his sleigh!
Talking like this they kept each other awake.
Now eleven o'clock, Charlie gave his duvet a shake.

"C'mon, Millie, we're going to get up, go down stairs and see
Santa come down the chimney with presents for you and me!"
And before another word could possibly be said,
Charlie and Millie had jumped out of the bed.

Charlie gathered Millie up and opened the door,
Silently tip-toeing across the landing floor.
No noise was made as the stairs were done,
For he made sure he avoided the squeaky one!

The door handle of the lounge he turned with care,
Slowly entering in case Santa was there.
They looked around the room, their eyes open wide,
And saw Charlie's stocking on the fireplace side.

(Sally's stocking wasn't there, for she had said
She preferred to have it at the end of her bed.)
On a plate in the front were two mince pies,
And some beer for Santa as a surprise.

Charlie and Millie settled down to wait,
Both of them in an excitable state.
They cuddled up together, nice and snug,
Sitting in the middle of the round mauve rug.

They stared at the fireplace, hoping to see
Santa appear miraculously.
They both grew sleepy as they did watch and wait,
Cuddled up together by the fireplace grate.

Their eyelids were heavy, and both gave sighs.
Too soon this pair had closed their eyes.
They dreamt of Santa in his suit of red
With reindeer pulling a present-loaded sled.

It seemed to Charlie as he watched Santa's face
That he had seen it before in another place.
It was familiar, friendly and gave him good cheer,
And then Santa said, "Thanks for the beer!"

Santa speaking woke them both from their dream.
They looked at each other, and Charlie said with a scream,
"He's been! Look at my stocking! He's been here!
Look at the floor! – Presents everywhere!"

But Millie had missed Santa and so shed a tear,
So Charlie said, "Don't worry – we'll do this next year!"

The Christmas Riddle

Christmas morning, and Charlie was full of glee,
For he'd just opened all but one present by the tree.
Sally and Charlie were seated on the ground
With dozens of unwrapped presents scattered all around.
There was a train, a ball, some socks, a book and shirt,
And for Sally, some shoes, puzzles, a dolly and a skirt.

Mum and Dad had opened some as well,
Sitting, smiling and content, one could tell.
Charlie and Sally had such a restless night
And opened their stockings early with delight.
"This was the bestest day in the whole year!"
For Santa had come! It was quite clear!

Charlie gave the last unopened present a lingering look.
"What could it be?" And in his excitement, he took
The last present, and the wrapping he did quickly unfold,
Revealing a long red box tied up with a ribbon of gold.
Under the ribbon was a note, which he took without delay.
The note said: "Inside's a Christmas Riddle for you today.
Solve the riddle, and you will very soon be
Seeing the very best present you'd hope to see!"
"What have you got?" Sally did ask.
"I've got a puzzle to solve and a task!"

So saying, he tore off the ribbon, took the lid off the box.
Inside was a folded note and a couple of his socks.
He expected the note, that was true,
But two socks? – Oh dear! He hadn't a clue!

He quickly read the little note,
And this is what someone wrote:
"Just a riddle for you, Charlie, at Christmas time,
And please forgive our little rhyme.

You must solve this puzzle and don't be slow.
Where first must these two blue socks go?"
Strange! thought Charlie, the rhyme complete,
"Surely socks must go on my own two feet!"
Sally said, "Yes, but before you put them on,
They go in the sock drawer, don't they? C'mon!"

Mum and Dad smiled as out of the room they did go.
Sally ran up the stairs with Charlie in tow.
They entered Charlie's bedroom and went to the chest.
"Puzzles are good," said Charlie. "They're what I like best!"
They looked at the sock drawer. "You open it!" Sally said.
"Alright!" said Charlie. "You sit on the bed!"

Charlie pulled the sock drawer slowly out
And looking in the drawer, let out a shout.
"I've got another note! What a game to play!"
"Oh stop messing about! What does it say?"
Charlie read, "Another clue – all in rhyme:
Where outside, can you tell the time?"
"I know this one!" said Charlie. "Come on, follow me!"
They rushed out of the room as fast as could be.

Across the landing, down the stairs, jumping the last two,
Made for the front door and quickly went through.
Now the garden outside was covered in snow,
But that didn't matter to these two, you know.
In the middle of a snowy lawn, Charlie stopped for a while.
He'd found the object of his search – a stone sundial!

"It's got to be under this snow!" he said, brushing some aside.
"Help me, Sal! Clear some snow! It has to be here!" he cried.
Together they cleared snow away.
Under the snow a little note lay.

"I knew it!" said Charlie. Sally jumped for joy.
"Another riddle," said this little boy.
"It says the last of our riddles is now here,
Find the solution and the rest will be clear.
The best Christmas present will be found
Underneath steps, but not underground!"

"This has got me puzzled, I have to say!"
"Me too!" said Sally. "But we have to find a way!"
"Hang on!" said Charlie. "I've got an idea.
Steps are stairs, aren't they? That's quite clear.
The object of our search – I think you will agree –
Will be under the stairs, don't you see?"
They looked at each other and then turned and ran.
Sally said, "Let's get to the stairs as fast as we can!"

Never so fast had both of them run.
These riddles were good and also fun!
Across the snow and through the front door,
Wiped their shoes on the mat and kicked off all four.
At the cupboard under the stairs they could only stare,
Wondering what the best present was, and what would be there.
Charlie turned the cupboard handle. Their hearts were beating fast.
Opened the cupboard slowly to reveal the present at last.

Both he and Sally could not believe their eyes.
For all the Ark animals were there and they shouted, "Surprise!"
There was whistle blowing, laughter, balloons and fun,
And for Charlie and Sally, well – the fun had just begun.
Charlie thought for a while and smiled, for he could now see
His friends would always be the best present there could be!

Charlie's Ark Animals

Flo the Cow

Hoff the Elephant

Snips the Cat

Drake the Duck

Pee the Dog

Red the Fox

Millie the Panda

Putty the Monkey

Scrump the Kangaroo & Joey

Gray the Owl

Em the Giraffe

Spout the Whale

Spud the Hippo

Zeep the Zebra

Splash the Dolphin

Charlie's Ark Animals

Ben the Mouse

Buss the Lion

Tumble the Penguin

Hayes the Pig

Fizzy the Hen

Jess the Sheep

Gee the Horse

Ace the Polar Bear

Geoff the Frog

Tex the Rabbit

Sam the Tiger

Puddle the Koala

Sy the Goose

Jay the Parrot

Mollie the Meercat

ABOUT THE AUTHOR

Award-winning international cartoonist and illustrator Mike Payne is perhaps best known as the creator and original artist of Tatty Teddy – the charcoal bear with the blue nose – from the Me To You concept, which he drew under the pen name of 'Miranda' for 17 years. He is also the creator of highly successful cartoon characters and licensed merchandise known across the world. It is estimated that greetings cards featuring his creations have sold in excess of one billion worldwide.

Mike has just illustrated and published his first children's story, *Milo's Lucky Sneeze*, along with a coffee table book of the first 120 cartoons he created about a little girl, Little Else, to raise people's spirits during lockdown.

As a child, Mike was always drawing, inspired by Disney and Giles, but ended up spending 26 years in the civil service. When the art director of Athena International happened upon an open portfolio of Mike's cartoons, Athena bought it all, and his career as a cartoonist was launched. When asked to create a bear with great depth of feeling for the then newly formed company Carte Blanche in 1987, it was then that he created the phenomenon that was Tatty Teddy, winning numerous awards in the USA, Europe, Scandinavia, Australia, New Zealand, South Africa and, of course, the UK. He won the equivalent of an Oscar, called a 'Henry', for his artwork, and has travelled the world attending many signings. He was also cartoonist for Sky News – the perfect environment to entertain and promote the art of cartooning for which he is globally renowned.

Mike created *Charlie's Ark* in June 2004, after waking up at 3.30am with a poem going round and round in his head about a five-year-old boy named Charlie and his ark-shaped toy box full of animals. He got up, went straight to his art studio and started writing and drawing, and the book and the audio CDs – which Mike narrated – were born. There are 24 stories in book one of *Charlie's Ark*, and Mike is still writing, inspired by the nostalgia and the moral in each of Charlie's adventures with the animals in his magical ark.

A
hug
is
a
wonderful
thing

Wishes
can
come
true

Every
day
is
an
adventure

The magic starts here